For my daughter, Isla
—C.N.

To Amelia
—A.A.

Let's Be Friends

By Caroline Ness
Illustrated by Alex Ayliffe

When Zack first
met Lucy he
hissed and spat.
He sharpened
his claws and
arched his back.

Each day he tried
to slip away,

to find a peaceful
dog-free place.

But Lucy wiggled and wriggled and wagged her tail,

and never left
poor Zack alone.

One night, when it was very cold,
Lucy crept toward Zack.
They curled together, head to tail,
and now they always sleep like that.

This morning
Lucy learned how to fish.

Zack climbed a tree
in the afternoon.

Then they chased butterflies together.

Tonight they're howling
at the moon.